Super SCRABBLE® BRAND FUN

Primary

Ages 6 to 8

Making Words
Starting Blends
Building Math Skills

Developed by the National SCRABBLE® Association

HOUGHTON MIFFLIN

Boston

MAKING WORDS

In *MAKING WORDS*, your child will be introduced to phonograms. Phonograms are simple letter groups made of a vowel sound and a consonant sound, such as *-at*. When a consonant or a consonant blend is added to the beginning of a phonogram, a word is made. If we add the consonant *b* to *-at*, for example, we get the word *bat*. If we add the consonant blend *fl* to *-at*, we get *flat*. Recognizing phonograms and the sounds they stand for is a basic decoding skill at the foundation of reading.

On these pages, your child will

P Phonograms — Identify the sound represented by a phonogram

R Reading — Decode words that contain phonograms

W Writing — Write words created with basic phonograms

A Anagrams — Unscramble a group of letters to make a word. An anagram is a word that's spelled with the exact same letters as another word. (Example: THICKEN and KITCHEN.)

-E₁ T₁

★ Look at the picture. Say the word. Write the word.

jet

pet

net

wet

★ Look at your SCRABBLE® tiles. Find the letters you see in the words above. On the table, make each word using the tiles.

W₄ E₁ T₁

P₃ Recognize the phonogram -et   S₁ Recognize the sounds represented by the letters J, P, N, W   W₄ Write the words jet, pet, net, wet

⭐ Look at your SCRABBLE® tiles. Find these letters: E, T, M, P, L, B, G. Read each sentence. Use your tiles to unscramble each word. Write the word.

-E₁ T₁

T₁ E₁ M₃   1. Pat _____ Pam.

E₁ P₃ T₁   2. Pam has a new _____ .

L₁ T₁ E₁   3. Pam will _____ Pat hold him.

T₁ E₁ B₃   4. I _____ Pam and Pat have fun.

G₂ T₁ E₁   5. Pat will _____ a pet too.

⭐ In the letter maze, find the words you wrote. Circle them. The letters that remain tell the name of Pam's new pet.

H	I	S	G	E	T	L
P	☐	N	A	M	E	E
E	M	E	T	I	S	T
T	B	E	T	J	E	T

-U₁ N₁

★ Look at the picture. Say the word. Write the word.

bun

run

sun

fun

★ Look at your SCRABBLE® tiles. Find the letters you see in the words above. On the table, make each word using the tiles.

B₃ U₁ N₁

P₃ Recognize the phonogram *-un* **S₁** Recognize the sounds represented by the letters *B, R, S, F* **W₄** Write the words *bun, run, sun, fun*

★ Read each clue. Write the word in the crossword puzzle.

-U₁ N₁

Down

1. The 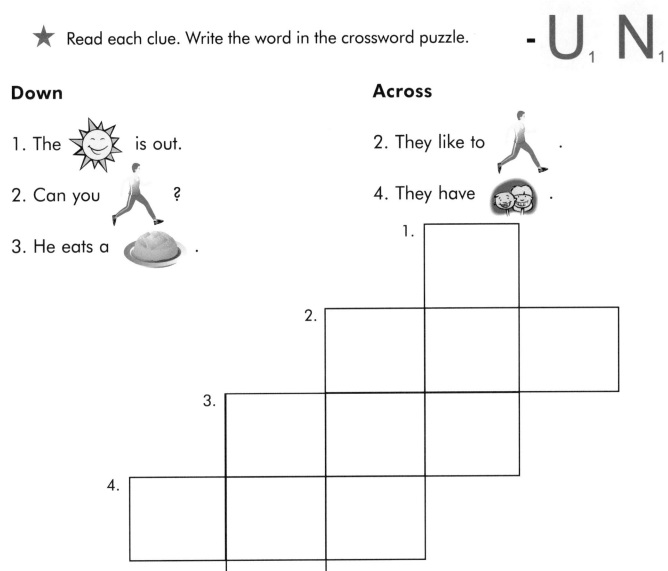 is out.

2. Can you ___ ?

3. He eats a ___ .

Across

2. They like to ___ .

4. They have ___ .

★ Look at your SCRABBLE® tiles. Find the letters in each word you wrote in the puzzle above. Place the letters UN on the last two squares. Make new words by placing different letters in front of UN.

U₁ N₁

- E₁ T₁ - U₁ N₁

★ What new pet did you get? Read each word. If the word rhymes with *met*, color the space around it blue. If the word rhymes with *pun*, color the space around it orange.

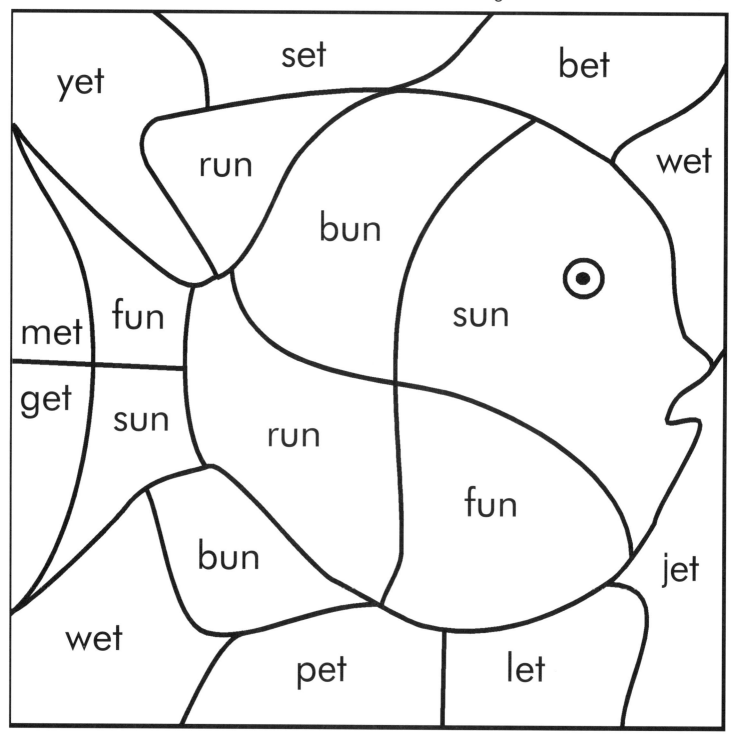

Look at each picture. Say the word. Put the two word parts together. Write the new word. Read the word you wrote.

-A₁ G₂

1. B₃ + A₁ G₂ = _____

2.  T₁ + A₁ G₂ = _____

3. W₄ + A₁ G₂ = _____

★ Look at your SCRABBLE® tiles. Find the letters you see in the words above. On the table, make each word using the tiles. Try putting other letters in front of AG to make other words.

S₁ A₁ G₂

P₃ Recognize the phonogram -ag   W₄ Write the words bag, tag, wag   S₁ Recognize the sounds represented by the letters W, S, B, T   R₁ Read

★ Look at each picture. Say the name. Find the letter pair that rhymes with the name of the pictured object. Circle them. Write them on the line to complete the word.

1.

ag
un
et

s _____

2.

et
ut
un

j _____

3.

un
et
ag

b _____

4.

ag
ut
un

t _____

5.

ag
ut
un

b _____

6.

un
ag
ut

w _____

P₃ Recognize the phonograms -un, -et, ag   W₄ Write the words *wag, bun, jet, tag, bag, sun*

★ Look at the picture. Say the word. Write the word. Read each
word you write.

-A₁ M₃

1. jam

2. ham

3. ram

4. yam

5. dam

★ Look at your SCRABBLE® tiles. Find the letters you see in the words above. On the table, make
each word using the tiles.

J₈ A₁ M₃

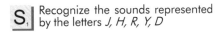

P₃ Recognize the
phonogram -am

S₁ Recognize the sounds represented
by the letters J, H, R, Y, D

W₄ Write the words jam, ham,
ram, yam, dam

R₁ Read

★ Look at your SCRABBLE® tiles. Find these letters: A, B, H, J, M, N, S, U, and Y. Read each sentence. Use your tiles to unscramble each word. Write the word to complete each sentence.

A₁ S₁ M₃   1. This is _____ .

J₈ M₃ A₁   2. Sam gets some _____ .

M₃ A₁ H₄   3. Sam eats some _____ .

M₃ A₁ Y₄   4. Sam gets a _____ .

★ What does Sam have? In the letter maze, find the words you wrote. Circle them. The letters that remain tell what Sam has. Write your answer below.

A S A M L O T

J A M Y A M T

O H A M E A T

Sam has ___ ___ ___ ___ ___ ___ ___ ___ ___!

P₃ | Recognize the phonogram -am   S₁ | Recognize initial consonant sounds S, J, H, Y   W₄ | Write the words *Sam, jam, ham, bun, yam*   A₁ | Solve anagrams

-AG -AM -ET -UN

⭐ Read each saying on the left. Draw a line from the saying to the picture it describes.

1. a bag in the sun

2. a pet in a net

3. a ram with a yam

4. jam on a bun

5. a tag on a jet

⭐ Use your SCRABBLE® tiles to make your favorite word group above. Then draw your own picture. Write about it.

P₃ Recognize the phonograms -ag, -am, -et, -un W₄ Write R₁ Read

★ Look at each picture. Say the word. Put the two word parts together. Write the word. Read the word.

1. 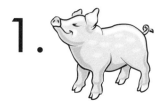 P₃ + = _____

2. W₄ + I₁ G₂ = _____

3.  D₂ + I₁ G₂ = _____

4. B₃ + I₁ G₂ = _____

★ Look at your SCRABBLE® tiles. Find the letters you see in the words above. On the table, make each word using the tiles. Try putting other letters in front of IG to make other words.

F₄ I₁ G₂

P₃ Recognize the phonogram -ig

W₄ Write the words *pig, wig, dig, big*

S₁ Recognize the sounds represented by the letters *P, W, D, B, F*

R₁ Read the words *pig, wig, dig, big*

★ Look at your SCRABBLE® tiles. Find these letters: I, G, W, P, J, D, B, F. Read each sentence. Use your tiles to unscramble each word. Write the word. Then read the sentence.

- I_1 G_2

G_2 I_1 W_4 1. Pat puts on a _____ .

I_1 J_8 G_2 2. Dan can do a _____ .

P_3 G_2 I_1 3. Can you pet a _____ ?

G_2 I_1 F_4 4. Jan has a _____ .

I_1 B_3 G_2 5. The cat is _____ .

G_2 I_1 D_1 6. The dog can _____ .

| P_3 Recognize the phonogram -ig | W_4 Write the words pig, wig, dig, big, fig, jig | S_1 Recognize the sounds represented by the letters P, W, S, B, J, T | R_1 Read |

★ Look at each picture. Say the name. Write the word.

1.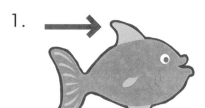

fin

2.

pin

3.

tin

4.

win

★ Look at your SCRABBLE® tiles. Find the letters you see in the words above. On the table, make each word using the tiles.

W₄ I₁ N₁

★ Look at your SCRABBLE® tiles. Find these letters: I, N, F, B, T, W, P. Read each sentence. Use your tiles to unscramble each word. Write the word to complete the sentence.

- I₁ N₃

N₁ I₁ B₃   1. Dan looks in the _____ .

P₃ N₁ I₁   2. Pat wins a _____ .

I₁ F₄ N₁   3. The fish has a _____ .

T₁ N₁ I₁   4. Did you see the _____ can?

I₁ W₄ N₁   5. Dan can _____ a pet.

★ In the letter maze, find the words you wrote. Circle them. In the spaces below, write the letters that remain to tell what kind of pet Dan won.

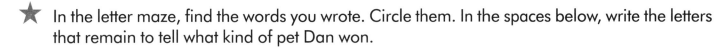

P	L	I	W	I	N
I	T	T	L	E	T
N	F	I	N	P	I
I	G	B	I	N	N

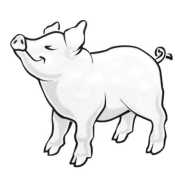

Dan won a   ___ ___ ___ ___ ___ ___   ___ ___ ___ .

P₃ Recognize the phonogram -in   S₁ Recognize initial consonant sounds B, P, F, T, W   W₄ Write the words pig, win, pin, bin, fin   A₁ Solve anagrams   R₁ Read

- I G - I N

★ What did your pet win at the fair? Read each word. If the word rhymes with *big*, color the space around it pink. If the word rhymes with *fin*, color the space around it blue.

- I₁ G₂ -A₁ G₂ -A₁ M₃
-E₁ T₁ - I₁ N₁

★ Read each saying on the left. Draw a line from the saying to the picture it describes.

1. a pig with a bag

2. a big dam

3. a pet with a fin

4. a ram with a tin

5. a wig with a tag

★ Use your SCRABBLE® tiles to make your favorite word group above. Then draw your own picture. Write about it.

- I₁ P₃

★ Look at each picture. Say the word. Write the word.

zip

dip

sip

rip

★ Look at your SCRABBLE® tiles. Find D, I, L, N, P, R, S, T, Z. Put IP on the table. Add a letter to the front to make a word. Read the word.

R₁ I₁ P₃

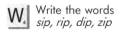

P₃ Recognize the phonogram -ip W₄ Write the words sip, rip, dip, zip S₁ Recognize the sounds represented by the letters D, L, N, P, R, S, T, Z R₁ Read

⭐ Look at each picture. Say the name. Find the letter pair that rhymes with the name of the pictured object. Circle it. Write it on the line to complete the word.

-I₁ P₃

1.

ig
ip
in

l _____

2.

ip
in
ig

z _____

3.

in
ip
ig

r _____

4.

ig
in
ip

t _____

5.

ig
in
ip

d _____

6.

ip
in
ig

s _____

P₃ Recognize the phonogram *-ip*   W₄ Write the words *sip, dip, lip, zip, tip, rip*

-O₁ B₃

★ Read each sentence. Put the two word parts together. Write the new word. Say the word.

1. This is **B₃** + **O₁ B₃** _____ .

2. She has a **J₈** + **O₁ B₃** _____ .

3. There is a **M₃** + **O₁ B₃** _____ .

4. I have a **C₃** + **O₁ B₃** _____ .

★ Look at your SCRABBLE® tiles. Find the letters you see in the words above. On the table, make each word using the tiles. Try putting other letters in front of OB to make other words.

J₈ O₁ B₃

P₃ Recognize the phonogram -ob	**S₁** Recognize the sounds represented by the letters C, M, B, J	**W₄** Write the words Bob, job, mob, rob	**R₁** Read

★ Look at your SCRABBLE® tiles. Find these letters: O, B, J, M, R, S. Read each clue. Use your tiles to unscramble each word. Write the word the clue describes.

- O_1 B_3

B_3 O_1 J_8 1. A work place. _____

O_1 B_3 B_3 2. A boy's name. _____

O_1 B_3 S_1 3. To cry hard. _____

B_3 M_1 O_1 4. A lot of people. _____

O_1 B_3 R_1 5. To steal something. _____

★ In the maze, find the words you wrote. Circle them. The letters that remain tell what Bob sells.

```
R   B   O   B   C   O   R   N   M

O   O   N   S   O   B   T   H   O

B   E   C   O   B   J   O   B   B
```

Bob sells ____ ____ ____   ____ ____   ____ ____ ____   ____ ____ ____ .

P_3 Recognize the phonogram -ob S_1 Recognize the sounds represented by the letters C, B, R, S, M, J W_4 Write the words *job, mob, rob, sob, Bob* A_1 Solve anagrams R_1 Read

⭐ Find these words in the maze. They are written across or down. Circle each word. Some letters will be used more than once. Write the remaining letters in order to solve the riddle.

rip	dip	nip	lip	zip
rob	cob	bob	job	sob	mob

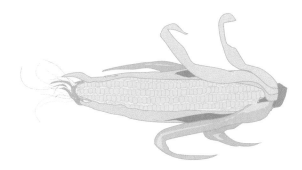

RIDDLE: I have teeth but no mouth. What am I?

R I P C N D I P

O O C Z I P B M

B M O B P J O B

S O B L I P B B

I am a ____ ____ ____ ____ .

★ Look at the picture. Say the word. Write the word.

-O₁ G₂

1.

log

2.

jog

3.

hog

4.

fog

★ Look at your SCRABBLE® tiles. Find the letters you used to begin the words above. Put OG on the table. Add each letter to the front of OG to make a word. Read each word. Try putting other letters in front of OG to make more words.

| **P**₃ | Recognize the phonogram -og | **S**₁ | Recognize the sounds represented by the letters B, F, H, J, L | **W**₄ | Write the words fog, hog, jog, log | **R**₁ | Read |

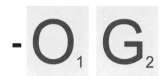

★ Look at your SCRABBLE® tiles. Find these letters: O, G, F, H, B, L, J. Read each sentence. Use your tiles to unscramble each word. Write the word to complete the sentence.

O_1 G_2 H_4 1. Jamie has a _____ .

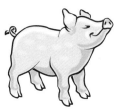

G_2 J_8 O_1 2. Jamie and his hog went for a _____ .

F_4 G_2 O_1 3. They ran in the rain and the _____ .

4. At the end of the jog, they sat down on

G_2 O_1 L_1 a _____ .

★ Read each sentence. Put the two word parts together. Write the new word. Say the word.

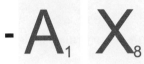

1. This is 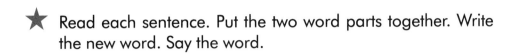 M₃ + A₁ X₈ _____ .

2. Max gets a F₄ + A₁ X₈ _____ .

3. He plays the S₁ + A₁ X₈ _____ .

4. He pays the T₁ + A₁ X₈ _____ .

★ Look at your SCRABBLE® tiles. Find the letters you see in the words above. On the table, make each word using the tiles. Try putting other letters in front of AX to make other words.

Find these words in the maze. They are written across or down. Circle each word. Write the remaining letters in order to solve the riddle.

fax	Max	lax	tax	wax	sax

RIDDLE: The more I dry, the wetter I get. What am I?

T A X I M

M L T F A

S A O A X

A X W X E

X L W A X

____'____ a ____ ____ ____ ____ ____ ____ .

What did Max get for his birthday? Read each word. If the word rhymes with *fog* color it blue. If the word rhymes with *tax* color it yellow.

 $-A_1$ X_8 $-O_1 G_2$

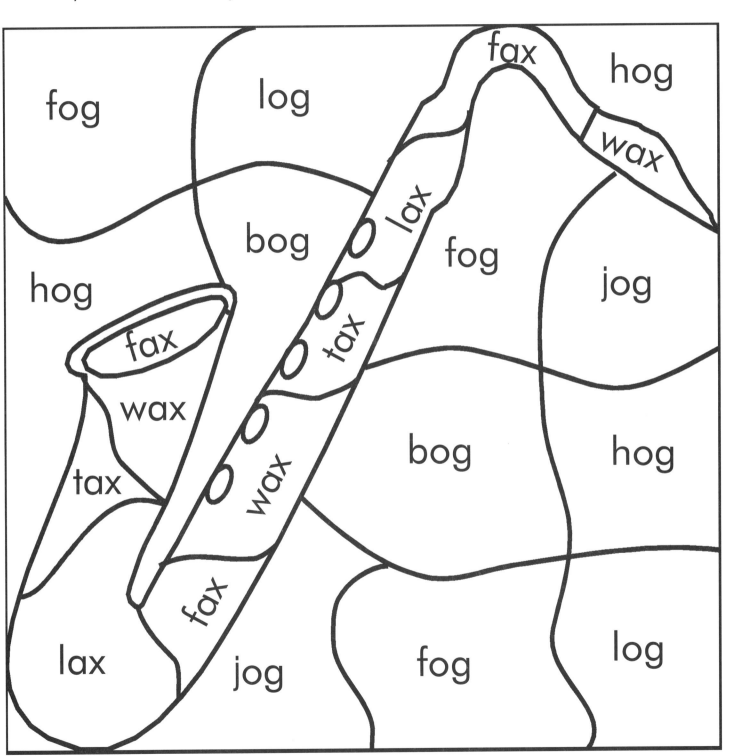

-U₁ M₃

★ Look at the picture. Say the word. Write the word.

yum

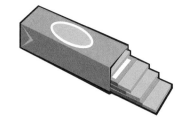

gum

hum

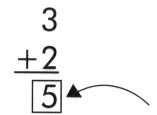

$$\begin{array}{r} 3 \\ +2 \\ \hline \boxed{5} \end{array}$$

sum

★ Look at your SCRABBLE® tiles. Find the letters you see in the words above. On the table, make each word using the tiles.

M₃ U₁ M₃

★ Look at your SCRABBLE® tiles. Find these letters: *H, U, M, G, S.* Read each clue. Use your tiles to unscramble each word. Write the word the clue describes.

- U₁ M₃

M₃ U₁ H₄   1. Singing without words.   ___ ___ ___
                                               1

U₁ S₁ M₃   2. Add two numbers to get this. ___ ___ ___
                                                4

M₃ U₁ G₂   3. You can chew this. ___ ___ ___
                                       3

M₃ Y₄ U₁   4. What you say when
                you see dessert.   ___ ___ ___
                                     2

★ Some letters above have numbers. Match each letter to its number below. Write the letters. The answer will tell you what everyones likes to get.

___ ___ ___ ___
 1   2   3   4

-U T

★ Look at each picture. Say the word. Put the two word parts together. Write the new word. Read the word.

1.  N + U T = _____

2.  C + U T = _____

3.  H + U T = _____

4.  R + U T = _____

★ Look at your SCRABBLE® tiles. Find the letters you see in the words above. On the table, make each word using the tiles. Try putting other letters in front of UT to make more words.

B U T

P₃ Recognize the phonogram -ut   W₄ Write the words *hut, nut, rut, cut*   S₁ Recognize the sounds represented by the letters *H, C, N, R*   R₁ Read

STARTING BLENDS

With **STARTING BLENDS,** your child will be introduced to initial consonant blends. Consonant blends are simply two or more consonants whose individual sounds blend together to make one sound. The consonant blend *fl-*, for example, blends the sounds represented by those two letters. When a consonant blend is added to the beginning of a phonogram, such as *–at,* we get *flat*. Recognizing consonant blends, phonograms, and the sounds they stand for is a basic decoding skill at the foundation of reading.

On these pages, your child will

B₃ Consonant Blends	Recognize initial consonant blends and the sounds they represent
R₁ Reading	Read words that contain initial consonant blends
W₄ Writing	Write words with initial consonant blends
P₃ Phonograms	Recognize common phonograms
A₁ Anagrams	Unscramble a group of letters to make a word. An anagram is a word that's spelled with the exact same letters as another word. (Example: THICKEN and KITCHEN.)
S₁ Sound/Symbol correspondence	Recognize sounds made by all 26 letters of the alphabet
C₃ Crossword Puzzle or word search	Apply new skills by solving puzzles

Blends: ch-, sh-

⭐ Blends are two letters whose sounds blend together to make one sound. Look at each picture. Say the name of the object. Circle **ch** if the word begins with the sound you hear in *chip*. Circle **sh** if the word begins with the sound you hear in *short*.

1.

ch   sh

2.

ch   sh

3.

ch   sh

4.

ch   sh

5.

ch   sh

6.

ch   sh

7.

ch   sh

⭐ Each sentence is missing a word. Complete each sentence by adding **ch-** or **sh-** to a letter group from the box. Write the word.

ade	ew	in	ow	ell	eep

1. The little chick says " _____ ."

2. Do you like the sun or the_____?

3. My dog likes to _____ a bone.

4. My class will put on a _____ .

5. He has whiskers on his _____ .

6. At the shore I found a pretty _____ .

MAKE WORDS!

⭐ Look at your SCRABBLE® tiles. Find these letter groups: **in, ip, ow, op,** and **eep**. Find **sh** and **ch**. Put **sh** and **ch** in front of each letter group to make words. Write the words you make on a separate sheet of paper. Here is an example:

⭐ Look at the first picture. Say the name of the object. Circle **fr** or **gr**. Then circle the picture whose name begins with the same sound.

1.          

fr   gr

2.          

fr   gr

3. 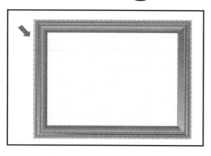         

fr   gr

4.         

fr   gr

★ Each rhyme is missing a word. The missing word rhymes with the underlined word. Complete each sentence with a word that begins with **fr-** or **gr-**.

1. It's an <u>ape</u> with a _____ .

2. I <u>came</u> to buy a _____ .

3. Look what I <u>found</u> on the _____ .

4. The _____ is on a <u>log</u>.

5. That _____ says "<u>Ouch</u>!"

6. The monkey <u>cries</u> for _____ .

MAKE WORDS!

★ Look at your SCRABBLE® tiles. Find these letter groups: **ank, in, ow, own,** and **ay**. Find **gr** and **fr**. Put **gr** and **fr** in front of each letter group to make words. Write the words you make on the lines below or use a separate sheet of paper. Here is an example:

F R A Y

1. _____   5. _____

2. _____   6. _____

3. _____   7. _____

4. _____

⭐ Look at each picture. Say the name of the object. Circle the letter in front of the correct blend. Write the blend to complete the word. The letter you circle will help you solve a riddle.

1.

i. ch
j. sh
k. gr

___ ___ ark

2.

s. gr
t. ch
u. fr

___ ___ og

3.

s. gr
t. fr
u. sh

___ ___ apes

4.

t. ch
u. fr
v. gr

___ ___ air

5.

r. ch
s. fr
t. sh

___ ___ ell

6.

g. gr
h. fr
i. ch

___ ___ ank

7.

p. sh
q. fr
r. ch

___ ___ art

8.

c. ch
d. fr
e. sh

___ ___ ip

9.

e. gr
f. fr
g. sh

___ ___ in

⭐ Solve this riddle. Write the letters of your answers in order below.

A man, his wife, and his son were driving to Orlando. At a gas station they met three families. Each family had a mother, father, and three children. How many people were going to Orlando?

___ ___ ___ ___   ___ ___ ___ ___ ___ !
 1   2   3   4   5   6   7   8   9

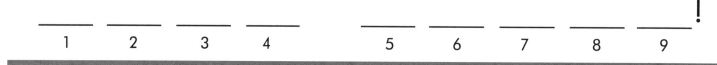

B₃ Consonant blends: recognize *ch-, sh-, fr-, gr-*   **R₁** Reading   **W₄** Writing   **P₃** Phonograms

Some pictures fell out of their boxes. Look at each box. Say the name of the object in each box. Say the name of each pictured object. Listen for starting blends that sound alike. Draw a line from each picture to the box it belongs in.

fl

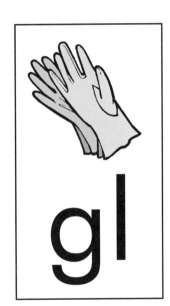

gl

⭐ Complete the crossword puzzle. Look at your SCRABBLE® tiles. Find tiles to match each set of letters below. Move the tiles around to make words that begin with **fl-** or **gl-**. Write each word you make in the correct square. Hint: Put **fl-** or **gl-** together first. Then move the other tiles around to make a word.

Down:

1. O_1 W_4 L_1 F_4

3. G_2 L_1 A_1 F_4

5. E_1 L_1 F_1 W_4

Across:

2. D_2 A_1 L_1 G_2

4. W_4 L_1 O_1 G_2

6. V_4 O_1 L_1 G_2 E_1

⭐ Look at each picture. Say the name of the object. Circle **br** if the word begins with the sound your hear in *bring*. Circle **cr** if the word begins with the sound you hear in *cry*.

1.

br   **cr**

2.

br   **cr**

3.

br   **cr**

4.

br   **cr**

5.

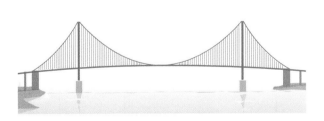

br   **cr**

6.

br   **cr**

7.

br   **cr**

B₃ Consonant blends: recognize *br-, cr-*   S₁ Sound/symbol correspondence

Complete the crossword puzzle. Look at your SCRABBLE® tiles. Find tiles to match each set of letters below. Move the tiles around to make words that begin with **br-** or **cr-**. Write each word you make in the correct square. Hint: Put **br-** or **cr-** together first. Then move the other tiles around to make a word.

Down:

1. R₁ O₁ W₄ C₃

3. C₃ B₃ A₁ R₁

5. B₁ I₁ C₃ R₁

Across:

2. D₂ E₁ A₁ B₂ R₁

4. W₄ O₁ R₁ B₂

6. D₂ I₁ A₁ B₃ R₁

⭐ The words in the box are hidden in the word maze below. The words are written across or down. Find each word. Circle it.

glue	globe	bread	broom	grass	glove	branch
	crab	crow	crib	crown		
grow	braid	flag	glow	brush	flower	flat

```
Q C R O W N O G D X T I
W Y E F L A T L R G B C
I L B A P F I U O L E F
B R U S H L R E M O Z E
R S I P T A G Q E V G M
A B Z D J G L O B E L C
N U B R O O M F A Z O R
C W Y O C R I B T U W A
H A B R A I D C G Q H B
J E G R O W B R E A D X
L G R A S S X O D F M T
F L O W E R L W B S N E
```

★ Some pictures fell out of their boxes. Look at each box. Say the name of the object in each box. Say the name of each pictured object. Listen for starting blends that sound alike. Draw a line from each picture to the box it belongs in.

sm sw

★ Each sentence is missing a word. Complete each sentence by adding **sm-** or **sw-** to a letter group from the box. Write the word.

ock	eet	all	im	eater	ile

1. I wear a _____ when I'm painting.

2. At the beach I like to _____ .

3. When it's cold I wear a _____ .

4. Your jokes make me _____ .

5. My feet grew so my shoes are too _____ .

6. This orange tastes _____ .

MAKE WORDS!

★ Look at your SCRABBLE® tiles. Find these letter groups: **ell, ear, eat, ay,** and **ash**. Find **sm** and **sw**. Put **sm** and **sw** in front of each letter group to make words. Write the words you make on the lines below or use a separate sheet of paper. Here is an example:

S M A R T

1. _____   5. _____

2. _____   6. _____

3. _____   7. _____

4. _____

B₃ Consonant blends: recognize *sm-, sw-*   R₁ Reading   W₄ Writing   P₃ Phonograms

Blends: sk-, sl-

★ Look at the first picture. Say the name of the object. Circle **sk** or **sl**. Then circle the picture whose name begins with the same sound.

1. **sk**   **sl**

2. **sk**   **sl**

3. **sk**   **sl**

4. **sk**   **sl**

★ Each rhyme is missing a word. The missing word rhymes with the underlined word. Complete each sentence with a word that begins with **sk-** or **sl-**.

1. We have a <u>date</u> to _____ at the pond.

2. Because of the <u>snow</u> we had to go _____ .

3. Do not _____ or you might <u>trip</u>.

4. Skating is a <u>thrill</u>, but it takes _____ .

5. We put our _____ under the <u>bed</u>.

6. When we go to _____
   we won't need to count <u>sheep</u>.

MAKE WORDS!

★ Look at your SCRABBLE® tiles. Find these letter groups: **in, ull, ip, y,** and **ate**. Find **sk** and **sl**. Put **sk** and **sl** in front of each letter group to make words. Write the words you make on the lines below or use a separate sheet of paper. Here is an example:

S₁ L₁ I₁ C₃ E₁

1. _____   5. _____

2. _____   6. _____

3. _____   7. _____

4. _____

B₃ Consonant blends: recognize *sk-, sl-*   **R₁** Reading   **W₄** Writing   **P₃** Phonograms

⭐ Look at each picture. Say the name of the object. Circle the letter in front of the correct blend. Write the blend to complete the word. The letters you circle will help you solve a riddle.

1.
w. sw
x. sm
y. sl

___ ___ eater

2.
h. sl
i. sm
j. sw

___ ___ oke

3.
s. sk
t. sl
u. sm

___ ___ i

4.
a. sw
b. sm
c. sl

___ ___ eeve

5.
m. sm
n. sk
o. sl

___ ___ ice

6.
n. sm
o. sk
p. sw

___ ___ ile

7.
q. sh
r. sw
s. sk

___ ___ irt

8.
i. sw
j. sk
k. sl

___ ___ an

9.
n. sk
o. sl
p. sw

___ ___ ate

⭐ Solve this riddle. Write the letters of your answers in order below.

Suppose you live in Wisconsin in the year 2002. You get into a time machine and go back 502 years. Where would you be?

___ ___ ___ ___ ___ ___ ___ ___ ___
1   2   3   4   5   6   7   8   9

★ This is a review page. The words in the box are hidden in the word maze below. The words are written across or down. Find each word. Circle it.

brain	chair	creek	flew	frog	from
glob	glue	grain	share	skill	slab
sling	small	swamp	sweet		

```
A  C  R  E  E  K  A  B  S  C  S  L
B  F  R  O  G  D  G  A  W  S  W  O
S  L  G  L  O  B  R  E  E  K  A  N
L  E  H  S  S  H  A  R  E  I  M  C
I  W  F  L  A  I  I  J  T  L  P  H
N  B  R  A  I  K  N  L  M  L  N  A
G  N  O  B  R  A  I  N  P  Q  O  I
D  S  M  A  L  L  G  L  U  E  P  R
```

★ Some of the pictures fell out of their boxes. Look at each box. Say the name of the object in each box. Say the name of each pictured object. Listen for starting blends that sound alike. Draw a line from each picture to the box it belongs in.

Complete the crossword puzzle. Look at your SCRABBLE® tiles. Find tiles to match each set of letters below. Move the tiles around to make words that begin with **dr-** or **pl-**. Write each word you make in the correct square. Hint: Put **dr-** or **pl-** together first. Then move the tiles around to make a word.

Down

1. N₁ D₂ K₅ I₁ R₁

3. L₁ P₃ M₃ P₃ U₁

5. R₁ W₄ A₁ D₂

Across

2. D₂ P₃ R₁ I₁

4. P₃ K₅ A₁ N₁ L₁

6. P₃ N₁ A₁ L₁

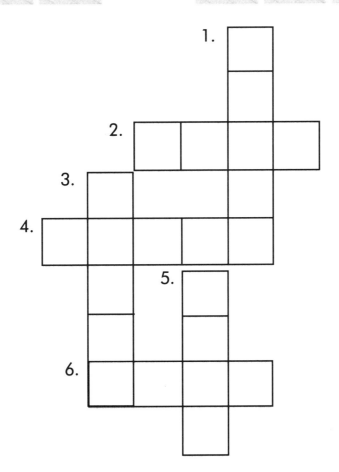

Blends: cl-, st-

★ Look at each picture. Say the name of the object. Circle **cl** if the word begins with the sound you hear in *club*. Circle **st** if the word begins with the sound you hear in *still*.

1.

cl   st

2.

cl   st

3.

cl   st

4.

cl   st

5.

cl   st

6.

cl   st

7.

cl   st

B₃   Consonant blends: recognize *cl-, st-*   S₁   Sound/symbol correspondence

★ Each rhyme is missing a word. The missing word rhymes with the underlined word. Complete each sentence with a word that begins with **cl-** or **st-**.

1. I can get <u>more</u> at the _____ .

2. That strange <u>duck</u> said, " _____ ."

3. Give me a <u>hand</u> so I can _____ .

4. He has <u>pep</u> in his _____ .

5. Tick <u>tock</u> went the _____ .

6. She likes to <u>play</u> with _____ .

MAKE WORDS!

★ Look at your SCRABBLE® tiles. Find these letter groups: **ump**, **amp**, **ick**, **one**, **uck**, and **ay**. Find **cl** and **st**. Put **cl** and **st** in front of each letter group to make words. Write the words you make on the lines below or on a separate sheet of paper. Here is an example:

S₁ T₁ O₁ R₁ Y₄

1. _____   5. _____   9. _____

2. _____   6. _____   10. _____

3. _____   7. _____   11. _____

4. _____   8. _____   12. _____

★ Read each sentence. Use your SCRABBLE® tiles to unscramble each word. Write the word. Remember that each word begins with **dr-**, **pl-**, **cr-**, **st-**, or **cl-**. Each circled letter will be used in the puzzle below.

O_1 U_1 L_1 D_2 C_1

1. There is not a ◯◯ _ _ _ in the sky.

R_1 V_4 D_2 I_1 E_1

2. Let's go for a _ _ _ _ _.

T_1 O_1 P_3 S_1

3. Can we _ _ ◯ _?

C_3 L_1 A_1 P_3 E_1

4. I know a good _ _ _ ◯_ to go.

O_1 E_1 T_1 S_1 R_1

5. It is a _ _ _ _ _.

K_5 R_1 I_1 N_1 D_2

6. I would like something to _ _ _ _◯.

★ Find SCRABBLE® tiles for each of the circled letters above. Unscramble them to solve the riddle.

RIDDLE: I have hands, but no fingers. I have a face, but no nose. What am I?

___ ___ ___ ___ ___

⭐ Look at the first picture. Say the name of the object. Circle **sc** or **sn**. Then circle the picture whose name begins with the same sound.

1.

   sc   sn

2.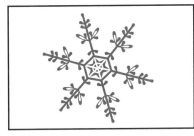

   sc   sn

3.

   sc   sn

4.

   sc   sn

B₃ Consonant blends: recognize *sc-, sn-*   **S₁** Sound/symbol correspondence

⭐ Each sentence is missing a word. Complete each sentence by adding **sc-** or **sn-** to a letter group from the box. Write the word.

eeze	old	ore	are	ail	ack

1. The team wants to _____ a few points.

2. Are you hungry for a _____?

3. This mask might_____ you!

4. I found a little _____ in the garden.

5. When I have a cold I _____ .

6. I_____ the dog when it takes my snack.

MAKE WORDS!

⭐ Look at your SCRABBLE® tiles. Find these letter groups: **ap, out, oop, ore, ail,** and **eer.** Find **sc** and **sn.** Put **sc** and **sn** in front of each letter group to make words. Write the words you make on the lines below or on a separate sheet of paper. Here is an example:

S₁ N₁ A₁ R₁ E₁

1._____   5. _____

2._____   6. _____

3._____   7. _____

4._____   8. _____

★ Look at the first picture. Say the name of the object. Circle **tr** or **tw**. Then circle the picture whose name begins with the same sound.

1.

   tr   tw

2.

   tr   tw

3.  **20   3 18**

   tr   tw

4.

   tr   tw

★ Each rhyme is missing a word. The missing word rhymes with the underlined word. Complete each sentence with a word that begins with **tr-** or **tw-**.

1. It's a _____ that is <u>stuck</u>.

2. Can you _____ your <u>wrist</u>?

3. There's a <u>skunk</u> in that _____ .

4. There's a <u>pig</u> near that _____ .

5. Those _____ have <u>grins</u>.

6. It's a <u>bee</u> in a _____ .

MAKE WORDS!

★ Look at your SCRABBLE® tiles. Find these letter groups: **ap**, **ig**, **ip**, **eat**, and **eet**. Put **tr** and **tw** in front of each letter group to make words. Write the words you make on the lines below or on a separate sheet of paper. Here is an example:

T R A P

1._____   4._____

2._____   5._____

3._____

⭐ Look at each picture. Say the name of the object. Circle the letter in front of the correct blend. Write the blend to complete the word. The letters you circle will help you solve a riddle.

1.
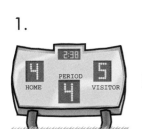

l. tr
m. sc
n. tw

__ __ ore

2.

a. tr
b. tw
c. sc

__ __ ick

3.
20

b. sc
c. sn
d. tw

__ __ enty

4.

e. sn
f. cl
g. tw

__ __ ail

5.
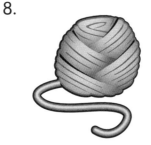

e. tw
f. tr
g. sc

__ __ arf

6.

k. sn
l. sc
m. tr

__ __ ale

7.

a. sn
b. sc
c. tr

__ __ owman

8.

r. cl
s. tw
t. tr

__ __ ine

9.

q. sn
r. sc
s. tr

__ __ eat

⭐ Solve this riddle. Write the circled letters of your answer in order below.

A red house is made of red bricks. A blue house is made of blue bricks. A yellow house is made of yellow bricks. What is a greenhouse made of?

It is ___ ___ ___ ___ of ___ ___ ___ ___ ___!
    1   2   3   4   5   6   7   8   9

B₃ Consonant blends: recognize sn-, sc-, tr-, tw-   **R₁** Reading   **W₄** Writing   **P₃** Phonograms

★ Some of the pictures fell out of their boxes. Look at each box. Say the name of the object in each box. Say the name of each pictured object. Listen for starting blends that sound alike. Draw a line from each picture to the box it belongs in.

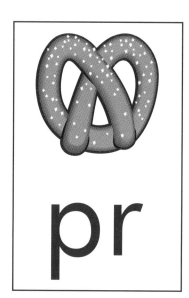

pr

bl

Complete the crossword puzzle. Look at your SCRABBLE® tiles. Find tiles to match each set of letters below. Move the tiles around to make words that begin with **pr-** or **bl-**. Write each word you make in the correct square. Hint: put **pr-** or **bl-** together first. Then move the other tiles around to make a word.

Down

1. C_3 R_1 I_1 P_3 E_1 I_1 P_3 E_1

3. M_3 O_1 L_1 O_1 B_3

5. L_1 U_1 R_1 B_3

Across

2. K_5 C_3 O_1 B_3 L_1

4. B_3 W_4 O_1 L_1

6. R_1 A_1 P_3 Y_8

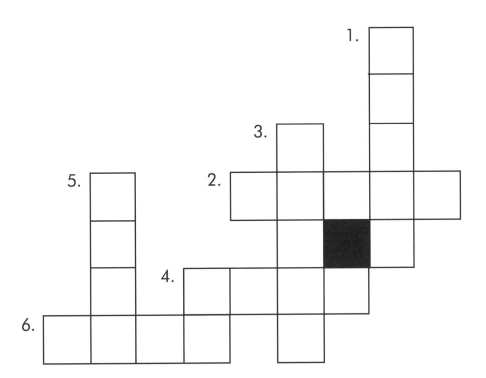

⭐ The words in the box are hidden in the word maze below. The words are written across or down. Find each word. Circle it.

tree	trunk	truck	train	prince
present	twin	twig	block	black
blanket	blue	pretzel	price	score
snail	trail	scar		

```
P   R   I   C   E   W   Q   T   W   I   G   Y
R   F   N   B   L   U   E   W   B   U   C   L
E   P   T   S   X   R   T   I   E   P   S   D
T   R   V   C   R   M   R   N   I   R   Z   I
Z   I   S   O   B   L   A   N   K   E   T   X
E   N   N   R   L   T   I   M   O   S   L   B
L   C   A   E   A   R   N   G   R   E   I   T
W   E   I   Z   C   E   D   B   C   N   D   R
A   B   L   D   K   E   B   L   U   T   W   U
Z   T   R   U   N   K   P   O   L   B   R   C
G   N   T   R   A   I   L   C   F   O   L   K
S   C   A   R   T   W   I   K   Z   U   X   E
```

Building M A T H Skills

Many people think that words are the most important aspect of the SCRABBLE® game. They're quick to recognize that playing the game requires vocabulary, spelling, and dictionary skills. What they often don't realize that math is an important part of the SCRABBLE® game that extends beyond basic score calculation. Yes, you have to find a word, but you also have to figure out where to play it. The word $C_3 A_1 T_1$ is not simply 5 points. If played through a Triple Word Score square it becomes 15. If the C_3 tile is placed on a Double Letter Score, the play earns 8 points.

Basic math skills are the foundation for being able to play the SCRABBLE® game and benefit from all the math exercises that experience encompasses, including addition, subtraction, multiplication, calculating without pencil and paper (mental math), spatial relationships, logic, and strategy. **Building Math Skills** will introduce or reinforce many of the primary level math skills used in the SCRABBLE® game to your child and also cover other important math topics they need to master.

On these pages, your child will

A_1 Practice basic addition

S_1 Practice basic subtraction

E_1 Learn estimation skills for 5, 10, and 20

P_3 Identify place value: ones and tens

T_1 Tell time to the hour, quarter hour, half hour, and three-quarter hour

M_3 Identify coin money; computation with coins

Addition

★ Count the figures in each picture. Write each number. Add them together. Write the sum.

1.  +  =

_____   _____   _____

2.  +  =

_____   _____   _____

3.  +  =

_____   _____   _____

4. 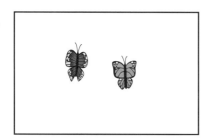 +  =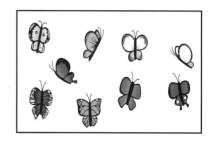

_____   _____   _____

5. 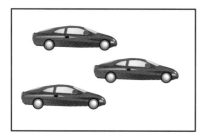 + 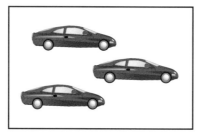 =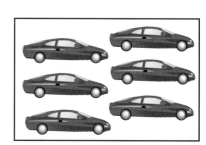

_____   _____   _____

A₁ Addition: Basic facts

★ This is the adding machine. Write the missing numbers. The first one is done for you.

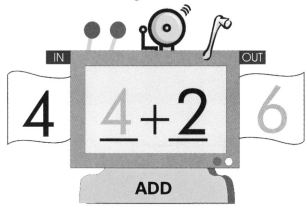

IN **4** | **4 + 2** | OUT **6** | ADD

1.

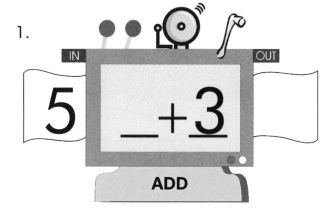

IN **5** | **_ + 3** | OUT | ADD

2.

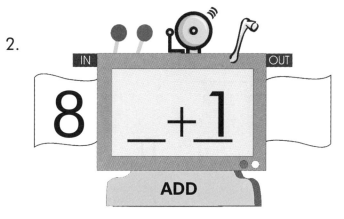

IN **8** | **_ + 1** | OUT | ADD

3.

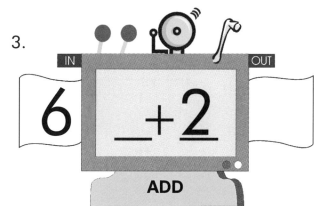

IN **6** | **_ + 2** | OUT | ADD

4.

IN **3** | **_ + 4** | OUT | ADD

5.

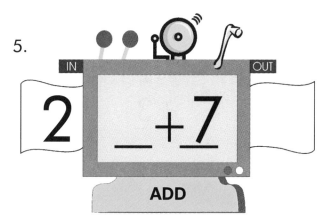

IN **2** | **_ + 7** | OUT | ADD

★ Put your own numbers in the machine. Write the answer.

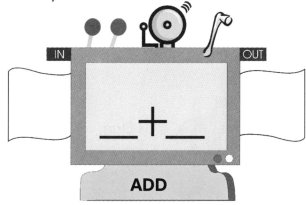

IN | **_ + _** | OUT | ADD

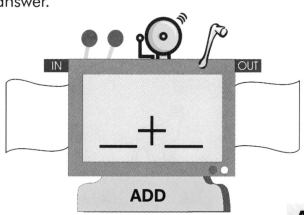

IN | **_ + _** | OUT | ADD

Addition: Basic facts **A**₁

Sometimes you do not have to count both numbers. You can add by counting on. Start with the biggest number. Count on the smaller number.

You have 5 cars. You get 3 more cars. How many cars do you have in all?
Start with 5. Count on 3. You have 8 cars in all.

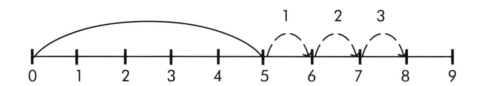

★ Add these numbers by counting on. Use the number line to help you. Start with the bigger number. Add on the smaller number. Write the sum.

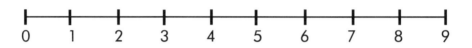

1.
$$5$$
$$+2$$

2.
$$4$$
$$+1$$

3.
$$3$$
$$+3$$

4.
$$6$$
$$+2$$

5.
$$0$$
$$+8$$

6.
$$3$$
$$+4$$

7.
$$7$$
$$+1$$

8.
$$2$$
$$+3$$

9.
$$4$$
$$+2$$

10.
$$3$$
$$+4$$

11.
$$6$$
$$+0$$

12.
$$4$$
$$+4$$

13. Dana read 3 s. Tanya read 2 more than Dana.

How many s did Tanya read?

_____ s

14. Dan walked 2 s. Jimmy walked the same number of s as Dan.

How many s did they walk in all?

_____ s

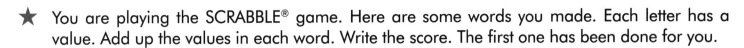

★ You are playing the SCRABBLE® game. Here are some words you made. Each letter has a value. Add up the values in each word. Write the score. The first one has been done for you.

1. C_3 A_1 T_1 3 + 1 + 1 = 5

2. O_1 F_4 F_4 _____

3. D_2 O_1 G_2 _____

4. S_1 A_1 N_1 D_2 _____

5. W_4 I_1 T_1 H_4 _____

6. B_3 U_1 G_2 _____

★ Get your SCRABBLE® tiles. Find the tiles in each row. Mix them around to make a word. Write the word. Write your score.

7. T_1 R_1 A_1 _____ ___ + ___ + ___ = ___

8. I_1 E_1 K_5 B_3 _____ ___ + ___ + ___ + ___ = ___

9. O_1 O_1 Z_{10} _____ ___ + ___ + ___ = ___

There are 6 balloons.
2 fly away.
How many balloons are left?

6 − 2 = 4

  6 balloons
  −2
  4 difference

There are 4 balloons left.

★ Write how many in all. Write how many are taken away. Subtract. Write the difference.

1.

_____ − _____ = _____ _____  s left.

2.

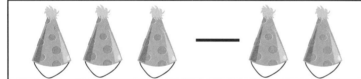

_____ − _____ = _____ _____ s left.

3.

_____ − _____ = _____ _____ s left.

4. Dan had 5 s.

 He gave Ben, Ed, and Jan one

  each.

 How many  s did Dan have left?

  _____ s left.

5. Pat had 7 s.

 She gave 2 s to Jill.

 She gave 3  s to May.

 How many s did Pat have left?

  _____ s left.

★ This is the subtraction machine. Write the missing numbers. The first one is done for you.

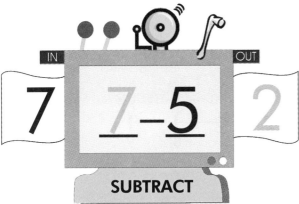

IN **7** | **7 – 5** | OUT **2**
SUBTRACT

1.
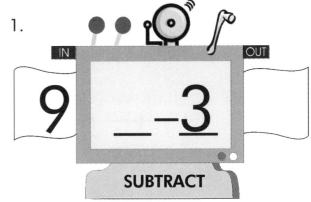

IN **9** | **__ – 3** | OUT
SUBTRACT

2.

IN **5** | **__ – 4** | OUT
SUBTRACT

3.
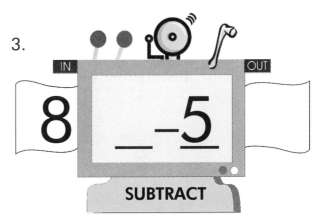

IN **8** | **__ – 5** | OUT
SUBTRACT

4.
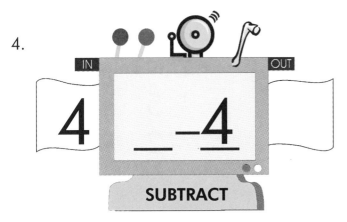

IN **4** | **__ – 4** | OUT
SUBTRACT

5.
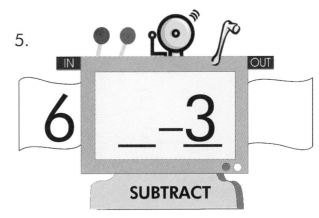

IN **6** | **__ – 3** | OUT
SUBTRACT

★ Put your own numbers in the machine. Write the answer.

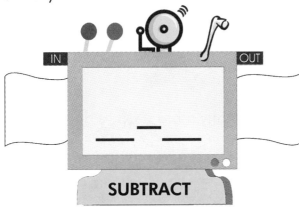

IN | **__ – __** | OUT
SUBTRACT

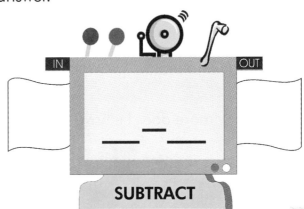

IN | **__ – __** | OUT
SUBTRACT

You can subtract by counting back.

You have 8 stickers. You put 2 stickers in your sticker book. How many stickers do you have left?
You have 8 stickers. Start at 8. Count back 2. You have 6 stickers left.

★ Subtract the numbers by counting back. Use the number line to help you.

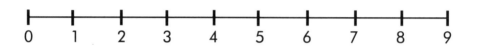

1.   7
   −2
_____

2.   6
   −1
_____

3.   5
   −1
_____

4.   8
   −3
_____

5.   4
   −2
_____

6.   7
   −3
_____

7.   8
   −2
_____

8.   5
   −3
_____

9.   4
   −1
_____

10. 9
   −3
_____

11. 5
   −2
_____

12. 7
   −1
_____

13. Dean took 4 s out of the library.

He read 3 s.

How many more does he have to read?

Dean has _____ s left to read.

14. Kim wants to collect all 9  s.

She has 2 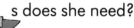 s so far.

How many more s does she need?

Kim has _____ s left to collect.

There are 8 little cars. Ned and Marcy share them. They play with the same number of cars.

8 – 4 = 4
4 + 4 = 8

Ned and Marcy each have 4 cars to play with.

★ Ned and Marcy share other things, and they always do it fairly. Draw pictures to show how they share. Write the addition and subtraction.

1.

Ned	Marcy

____ + ____ = ____

____ – ____ = ____

2.

Ned	Marcy

____ + ____ = ____

____ – ____ = ____

3.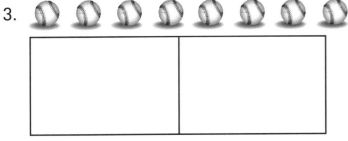

Ned	Marcy

____ + ____ = ____

____ – ____ = ____

4.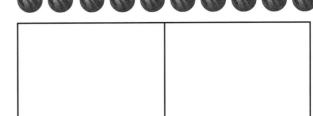

Ned	Marcy

____ + ____ = ____

____ – ____ = ____

Addition: Double facts **A**₁ Subtraction: Double facts **S**₁

S₁ T₁ F₄ U₁ A₁
D₂ B₃ P₃ H₄ X₈

This is ten.

This is ten.

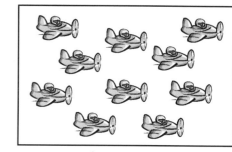

This is ten.

★ Look at the pictures in each row. Without counting, circle the picture that has about ten.

1.

2.

A₁	K₅	E₁	H₄
I₁	M₃	B₃	
U₁	N₁	S₁	J₈

A₁	R₁	K₅	F₄	E₁	M₃
I₁	Z₁₀	B₃	P₃	J₈	U₁
N₁	G₂	S₁	L₁	H₄	O₁

A₁			I₁
	K₅		
U₁			N₁

3.

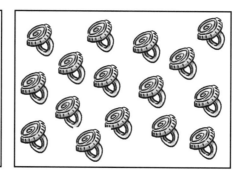

4.

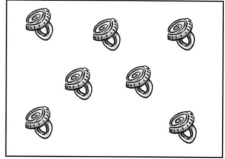

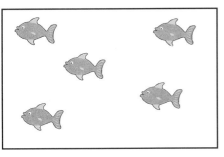

This is five.

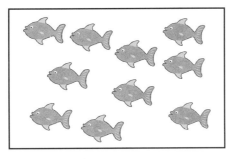

This is ten.

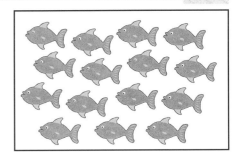

This is fifteen.

★ Look at each box below. Guess about how many fish are in each box. Circle the answer. Then write the letter of each answer below to answer the riddle.

1.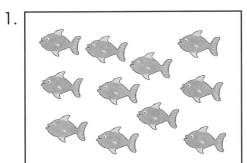

g. 10   h. 15

2.

n. 10   o. 5

3.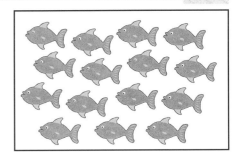

f. 15   g. 10

4.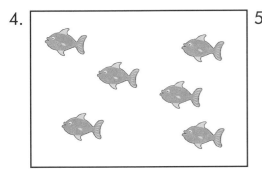

h. 10   i. 5

5.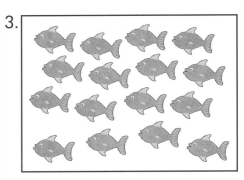

r. 10   s. 15

6.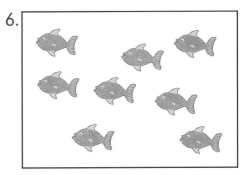

h. 10   i. 15

What game do sharks like to play?

___ ___   ___ ___ ___ ___
 1   2   3   4   5   6

Each rod has 10 cubes.

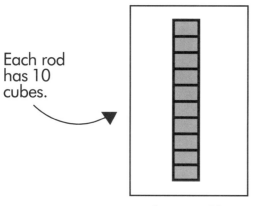

1 ten = 10

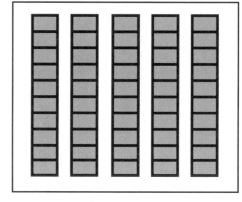

5 tens = 50

 Count the tens. Write the number.

1.

_____ tens = _____

2.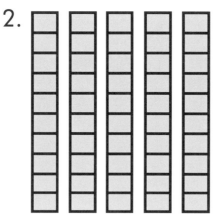

_____ tens = _____

3.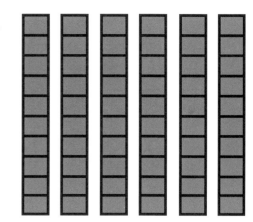

_____ tens = _____

4.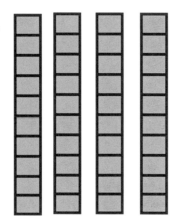

_____ tens = _____

5.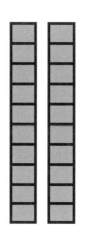

_____ tens = _____

6.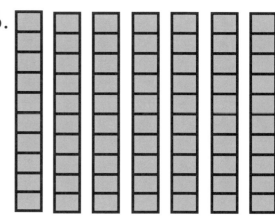

_____ tens = _____

A₁ Addition: Tens

 Each rod equals 10.

1. Color 2 tens.

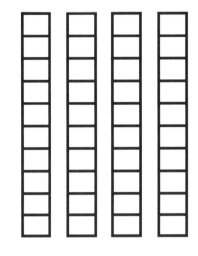

Write the number of squares. _____

2. Color 4 tens.

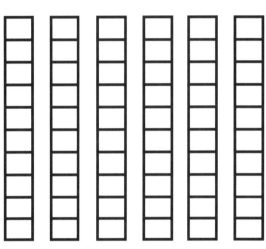

Write the number of squares. _____

3. Color 3 tens.

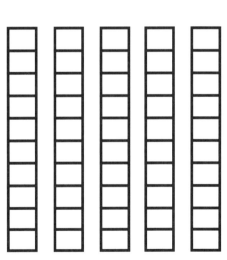

Write the number of squares. _____

4. How many did you color in all? _____ tens = _____ .

5. How many are not colored? _____ tens = _____ .

$$3 \quad \square\square\square$$
$$\underline{+4} \quad \blacksquare\blacksquare\blacksquare\blacksquare$$
$$7$$

You can add ones.
You can add tens.

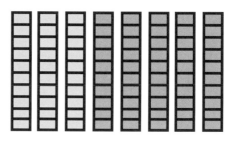

tens	ones
3	0
+5	0
8	0

★ Count how many cubes in all. First add the ones. Then add tens. Write the sum. Remember 0+0=0.

1.

tens	ones
3	0
2	0

_____

2.

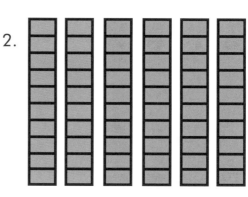

tens	ones
2	0
4	0

_____

★ Add the tens. Write the sum.

3.
$$50$$
$$\underline{+10}$$

4.
$$20$$
$$\underline{+40}$$

5.
$$60$$
$$\underline{+30}$$

6.
$$40$$
$$\underline{+40}$$

7.
$$30$$
$$\underline{+20}$$

8.
$$70$$
$$\underline{+20}$$

9.
$$10$$
$$\underline{+40}$$

10.
$$80$$
$$\underline{+10}$$

11.
$$40$$
$$\underline{+50}$$

12.
$$30$$
$$\underline{+40}$$

13.
$$20$$
$$\underline{+60}$$

14.
$$10$$
$$\underline{+70}$$

This is the ones place.

This is the tens place.

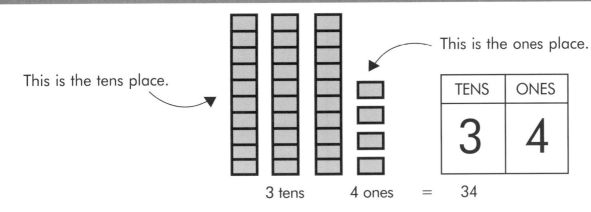

TENS	ONES
3	4

3 tens   4 ones   =   34

★ Count and write how many tens. Count and write how many ones. Write the number.

1.

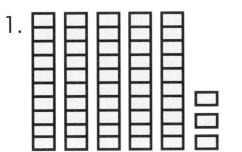 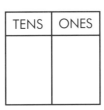

TENS	ONES

_____ tens _____ ones = _____

2.

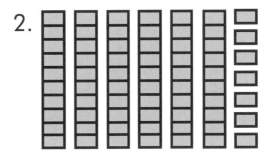

TENS	ONES

_____ tens _____ ones = _____

3.

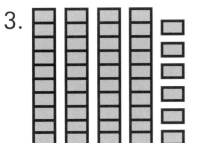

TENS	ONES

_____ tens _____ ones = _____

4.

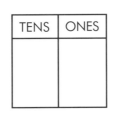

TENS	ONES

_____ tens _____ ones = _____

5.

TENS	ONES

_____ tens _____ ones = _____

6.

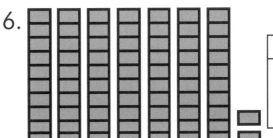

TENS	ONES

_____ tens _____ ones = _____

★ Color as many tens as you like. Color as many ones as you like. Use your favorite color. Write the number.

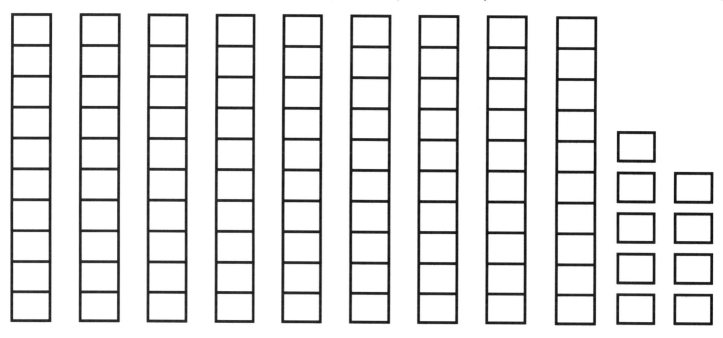

_____ tens _____ ones = _____

TENS	ONES

★ Look at each number. Write how many tens. Write how many ones.

1. 32 = _____ tens _____ ones

2. 46 = _____ tens _____ ones

3. 64 = _____ tens _____ ones

4. 81 = _____ tens _____ one

5. 19 = _____ ten _____ ones

6. 55 = _____ tens _____ ones

7. 27 = _____ tens _____ ones

8. 73 = _____ tens _____ ones

Penny 1¢
front   back

Nickel 5¢
front   back

Dime 10 ¢
front   back

1. Count the pennies. Write how much money you have.

_____ ¢

2. Count the nickels by five. Write the amount.

_____ ¢

3. Count the dimes by ten. Write the amount.

_____ ¢

★ Count the coins in each purse. Write how much money is in each purse.

4.

_____ ¢

5.

_____ ¢

★ Count the money in the box. Write how much. Look at the toys. Circle the one you could buy with the money.

1. _____ ¢

50¢   30¢   38¢

2. _____ ¢

25¢   45¢   35¢

3. _____ ¢

49¢   45¢   55¢

4. _____ ¢

65¢   Crayons 75¢   60¢

This is a penny.
It is worth 1¢.

 This is a nickel.
It is worth 5¢.

 This is a dime.
It is worth 10¢.

 This is a quarter.
It is worth 25¢.

 Count the money in each box. Write the amount. Then circle the piggy bank that has the same amount.

1. 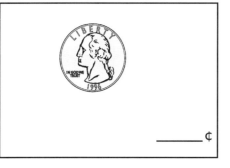 _____ ¢

2.  _____ ¢

3.  _____ ¢

4.  _____ ¢

Addition **A** Money **M**₃

Each day is divided into seconds, minutes, and hours. This is how we measure time.

The minute hand is long. It is at 12.

The hour hand is short. It is at 2.

There are 60 minutes in an hour. Each small line equals one minute.

It is 2 o'clock.
It is 2:00.

When the minute hand is at 6, the hour hand is between two numbers.

The minute hand is at 6.
The hour hand is between 2 and 3.

It is 2:30.
It is 30 minutes after 2.

★ Look at each clock. Write the time. The first one is done for you.

1.

___4___ o'clock

4:00

2.

_____ o'clock

_____

3.

_____ o'clock

_____

4.

_____ minutes after _____

_____

5.

_____ minutes after _____

_____

6.

_____ minutes after _____

_____

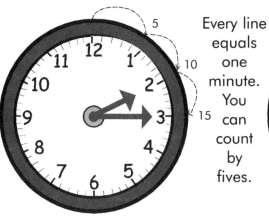

Every line equals one minute. You can count by fives.

It is 2:15.
It is 15 minutes after 2.
Two fifteen.

It is 2:30.
It is 30 minutes after 2.
It is half past 2. Two thirty.

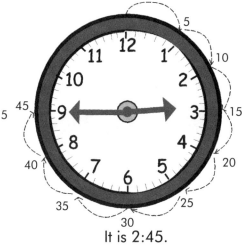

It is 2:45.
It is 45 minutes after 2.
Two forty-five.

★ Look at each clock. Write the time.

1.

_____ minutes after _____

_____

2.

_____ minutes after _____

_____

3.

_____ minutes after _____

_____

4.

_____ minutes after _____

_____

5.

_____ minutes after _____

_____

6.

_____ minutes after _____

_____

★   How do you spend your time? Look at the pictures. Draw the hands on the clock. Write the time.

1.

2.

3.

I wake up at_____:_____

I eat breakfast at_____:_____

I go to school at_____:_____

4.

5.

6.

I eat lunch at_____:_____

I do homework at_____:_____

I go to bed at_____:_____

TENS	ONES
▥▥	▭
2	2

+

TENS	ONES
▥	▭
1	6

=

TENS	ONES
▥▥▥	▭▭
3	8

★ Write down how many ones and how many tens are in the boxes. Add. Write the sum.

1.

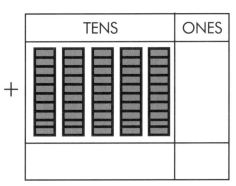   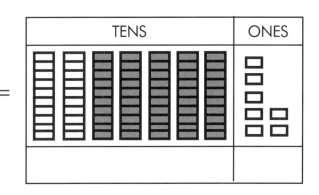

2.

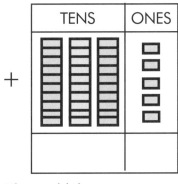   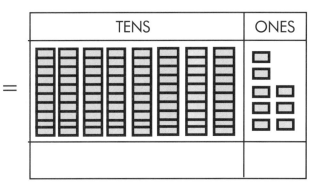

3.

★ Find the sum. Add the ones. Then add the tens.

4. $\begin{array}{r} 26 \\ +13 \\ \hline \end{array}$ 5. $\begin{array}{r} 64 \\ +22 \\ \hline \end{array}$ 6. $\begin{array}{r} 81 \\ +17 \\ \hline \end{array}$ 7. $\begin{array}{r} 32 \\ +25 \\ \hline \end{array}$ 8. $\begin{array}{r} 45 \\ +41 \\ \hline \end{array}$

Snowflake Addition

★ Add the number in the center of the snowflake to a number around it. Write the sum. The first one has been done for you.

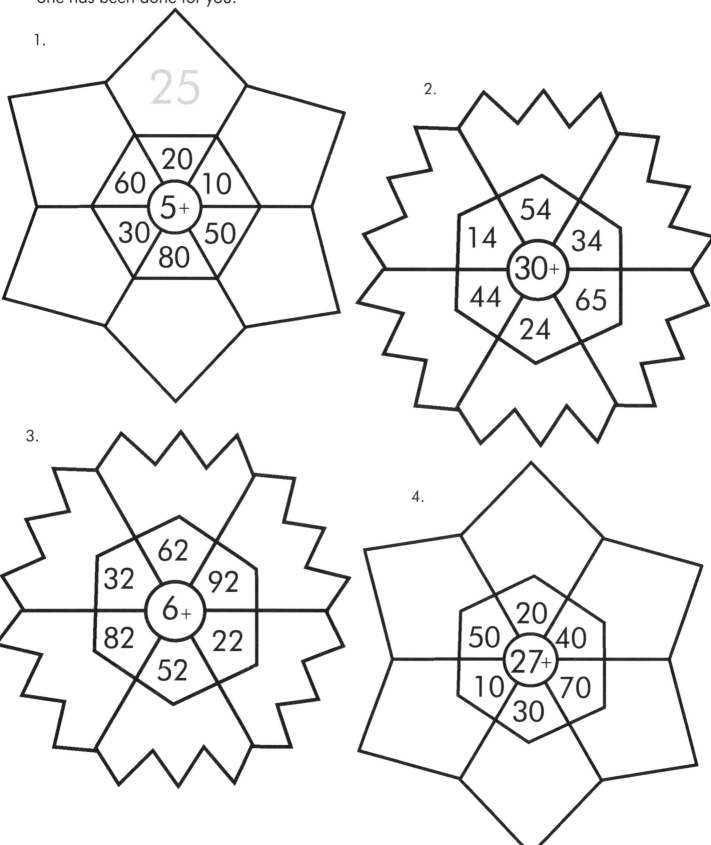

1.

25

20
60   10
5+
30   50
80

2.

54
14   34
30+
44   65
24

3.

62
32   92
6+
82   22
52

4.

20
50   40
27+
10   70
30

★ You are playing the SCRABBLE® game. Add up the points you score for each word. Add that to your total score.

1. Your score is ────────────────────→ **24**

   You play Q₁₀ U₁ I₁ L₁ T₁ for _____ points.

   Your new score is _____ .

2. Your score is ────────────────────→ **13**

   You play C₃ A₁ K₅ E₁ S₁ for _____ points.

   Your new score is _____ .

3. Your score is ────────────────────→ **21**

   You play J₈ A₁ C₃ K₅ S₁ for _____ points.

   Your new score is _____ .

4. Your score is ────────────────────→ **32**

   You play L₁ A₁ Z₁₀ Y₄ for _____ points.

   Your new score is _____ .

✎ Can you beat the scores above with the tiles on this rack? Find the highest-scoring word. Write it on the line.

Your score is 30.

A₁ E₁ K₅ O₁ O₁ Z₁₀ S₁

_____ = _____ points.

My new score is _____ .

Addition: 2-digit numbers A₁

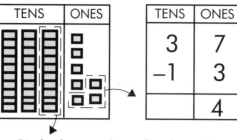

TENS	ONES
3	7
−1	3
	4

TENS	ONES
3	7
−1	3
2	4

$37-13=$ _____

First subtract the ones.
Then subtract the tens.

★ Look at each problem. Circle the number of rods and squares you need to subtract. Write the difference.

1. $26-15=$ _____

TENS	ONES

TENS	ONES
2	6
−1	5

2. $48-27=$ _____

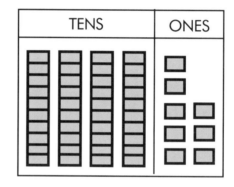

TENS	ONES
4	8
−2	7

3. $54-34=$ _____

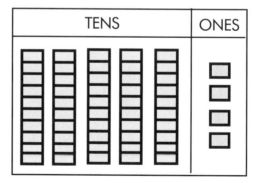

TENS	ONES
5	4
−3	4

★ Find the difference. Subtract the ones. Then subtract the tens.

4. 62	5. 46	6. 87	7. 32	8. 55
−21	−15	−64	−11	−34
_____	_____	_____	_____	_____

1.

★ Subtract a number in the outside circle from the number in the center. Write the difference. The first one is done for you.

2.

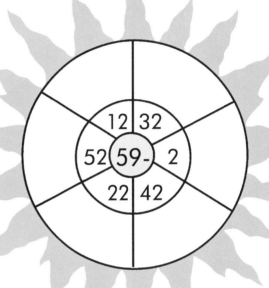

3.

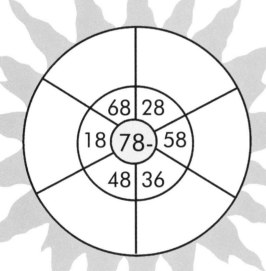

4.

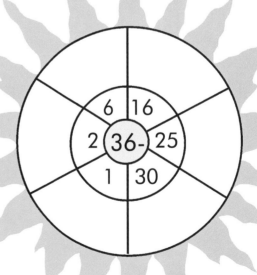

★ Read each problem. Write the answer in the space.

1. Dan and Rick are playing the SCRABBLE® game. Dan's score is 78. Rick's score is 62. How many points does Rick need to be tied with Dan?

_____

2. Rick scores 17 points. What is his score now? How many points is he ahead of Dan?

_____

3. Gina plays basketball. She has scored 53 points for her team this season. The record for points scored is 67. How many points does Gina need to tie the record? How many does she need to beat the record?

_____

4. Dion has 89 baseball trading cards. Jim has 77 cards. How many more cards does Dion have than Jim? Jim gets 12 more baseball cards. Who has more cards now?

_____

5. Wendy and Kate are playing the SCRABBLE® game. They are tied at 50 points each. Wendy scores 27 points. Kate scores 18 points. Who is ahead?

_____

6. There are 38 tiles missing from the SCRABBLE® game. Joel finds 14. His brother, Mike, finds 23. How many tiles are still missing? (Hint: Add. Then subtract.]

_____

R₁	A₁	Q₁₀	V₄	M₃
B₃	W₄	G₂	O₁	E₁
Z₁₀	C₃	S₁	F₄	N₁
P₃	H₄	T₁	I₁	L₁

This is twenty.

★ Look at the pictures in each row. Without counting, circle the picture that has about twenty.

1.

2.

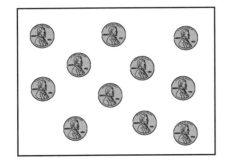 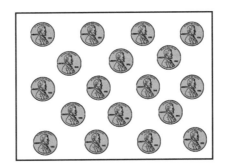 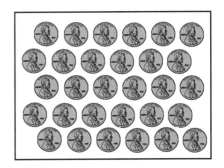

3.

4.

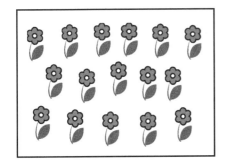 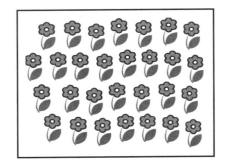 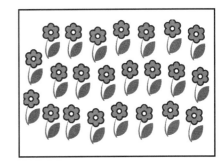

Estimation E₁

★ Read the following sentences. Make a good guess. Choose 5, 10, or 20. Write the answer in the space.

1.

I have about _____ cookies at snack time.

2.

I spend _____ hours each week playing.

3.

I spend _____ hours each week helping.

4.

I use _____ crayons to draw a picture.

5.

I read _____ books last month.

6.

It takes me _____ minutes to get to school.

5. 1. MET **2.** PET **3.** LET **4.** BET **5.** GET

Pet's name: JET

7. Down 1. SUN **2.** RUN **3.** BUN
   Across 2. RUN **4.** FUN

9. 1. BAG **2.** TAG **3.** WAG

10. 1. SUN **2.** JET **3.** BAG **4.** TAG **5.** BAG
   6. WAG

12. 1. SAM **2.** JAM **3.** HAM **4.** YAM

Answer: Sam has a lot to eat!

14. 1. PIG **2.** WIG **3.** DIG **4.** BIG

15. 1. WIG **2.** JIG **3.** PIG **4.** FIG **5.** BIG **6.** DIG

17. 1. BIN **2.** PIN **3.** FIN **4.** TIN **5.** WIN

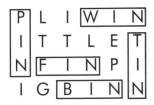

Answer: Dan won a little pig.

21. 1. LIP **2.** ZIP **3.** RIP **4.** TIP **5.** DIP **6.** SIP

22. 1. BOB **2.** JOB **3.** MOB **4.** COB

23. 1. JOB **2.** BOB **3.** SOB **4.** MOB **5.** ROB

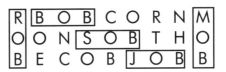

Answer: Bob sells corn on the cob.

24.

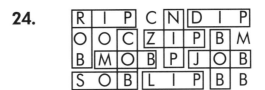

Answer: I am a comb.

26. 1. HOG **2.** JOG **3.** FOG **4.** LOG

27. 1. MAX **2.** FAX **3.** SAX **4.** TAX

28.

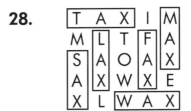

Answer: I'm a towel.

31. 1. HUM **2.** SUM **3.** MUG **4.** YUM

Answer: Hugs

32. 1. NUT **2.** CUT **3.** HUT **4.** RUT

Page 34: 1. sh **2.** ch **3.** ch **4.** sh **5.** sh **6.** ch **7.** sh

Page 35: 1. cheep **2.** shade **3.** chew **4.** show **5.** chin **6.** shell

MAKE WORDS

1. shin **2.** ship **3.** show **4.** shop **5.** sheep
6. chin **7.** chip **8.** chow **9.** chop **10.** cheep

Page 36: 1. fries **2.** grapes **3.** grade **4.** frog

Page 37: 1. grape **2.** frame **3.** ground **4.** frog **5.** grouch **6.** fries

MAKE WORDS

1. grin **2.** grow **3.** grown **4.** gray **5.** frank
6. frown **7.** fray

Page 38: 1. j.sh **2.** u.fr **3.** s.gr **4.** t.ch **5.** t.sh **6.** h.fr **7.** r.ch **8.** e.sh **9.** e.gr

RIDDLE: just three

Page 39: fl: flag, fly, flute **gl:** globe, glass, glue

Page 40: 1. flow **2.** glad **3.** flag **4.** glow **5.** flew **6.** glove

Page 41: 1. br **2.** cr **3.** cr **4.** br **5.** cr **6.** br **7.** br

Page 42: 1. crow **2.** bread **3.** crab **4.** brow **5.** crib **6.** braid

Page 43:

```
Q C R O W N O G D X T I
W Y E F L A T L R G B C
I L B A P F I U O G E F
B R U S H L R M O L Z E
R S I P T A G Q E V G M
A B Z D J G L O B E L C
N U B R O O M F A Z O R
C W Y O C R I B T U W A
H A B R A I D C G Q H B
J E G R O W B R E A D X
L G R A S S X O D F M T
F L O W E R L W B S N E
```

Page 44: **sm:** smock, smell, smoke
sw: sweater, sweep, swing

Page 45: **1.** smock **2.** swim **3.** sweater **4.** smile
5. small **6.** sweet

MAKE WORDS

1. smell **2.** smear **3.** smash **4.** swell **5.** swear
6. sweat **7.** sway

Page 46: **1.** skunk **2.** slipper **3.** skier **4.** sleep

Page 47: **1.** skate **2.** slow **3.** skip **4.** skill
5. sled **6.** sleep

MAKE WORDS

1. skin **2.** skull **3.** skip **4.** sky **5.** skate **6.** slip
7. sly **8.** slate

Page 48: **1.** w.sw **2.** i.sm **3.** s.sk **4.** c.sl **5.** o.sl
6. n.sm **7.** s.sk **8.** i.sw **9.** n.sk

RIDDLE: Wisconsin

Page 49:

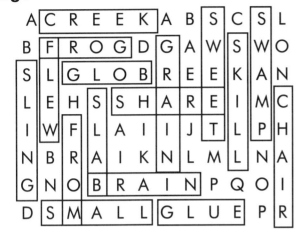

Page 50: **dr:** dress, dragon, drill
pl: plant, plug, plate

Page 51: 1. drink 2. drip 3. plump 4. plank
5. draw 6. plan

Page 52: 1. cl 2. cl 3. st 4. cl 5. st 6. st 7. cl

Page 53: 1. store 2. cluck 3. stand 4. step
5. clock 6. clay

MAKE WORDS

1. clump 2. clamp 3. click 4. clone 5. cluck
6. clay 7. stump 8. stamp 9. stick 10. stone
11. stuck 12. stay

Page 54: 1. cloud 2. drive 3. stop 4. place
5. store 6. drink

RIDDLE: clock

Page 55: 1. scale 2. snail 3. scoop 4. snowman

Page 56: 1. score 2. snack 3. scare 4. snail
5. sneeze 6. scold

MAKE WORDS

1. scout 2. scoop 3. score 4. snap 5. snout
6. snoop 7. snore 8. snail 9. sneer

Page 57: 1. twig 2. trick 3. twenty 4. trunk

Page 58: 1. truck 2. twist 3. trunk 4. twig 5. twins
6. tree

MAKE WORDS

1. trap 2. trip 3. treat 4. twig 5. tweet

Page 59: 1. m.sc 2. a.tr 3. d.tw 4. e.sn 5. g.sc
6. l.sc 7. a.sn 8. s.tw 9. s.tr

RIDDLE: It is made of glass!

Page 60: **pr:** present, prune, prize
bl: blue, blanket, blow

Page 61: 1. price 2. block 3. bloom 4. blow
5. blur 6. pray

Page 62:

P	R	I	C	E	W	Q	T	W	I	G	Y
R	F	N	B	L	U	E	W	B	U	C	L
E	P	T	S	X	R	T	I	E	P	S	D
T	R	V	C	R	M	R	N	I	R	Z	I
Z	I	S	O	B	L	A	N	K	E	T	X
E	N	N	R	L	T	I	M	O	S	L	B
L	C	A	E	A	R	N	G	R	E	I	T
W	E	I	Z	C	E	D	B	C	N	D	R
A	B	L	D	K	E	B	L	U	T	W	U
Z	T	R	U	N	K	P	O	L	B	R	C
G	N	T	R	A	I	L	C	F	O	L	K
S	C	A	R	T	W	I	K	Z	U	X	E

PAGE 64: 1. $1 + 3 = 4$ 2. $5 + 3 = 8$
3. $4 + 3 = 7$ 4. $2 + 7 = 9$
5. $3 + 3 = 6$

PAGE 65: 1. $5 + 3 = 8$ 2. $8 + 1 = 9$
3. $6 + 2 = 8$ 4. $3 + 4 = 7$
5. $2 + 7 = 9$

PAGE 66: 1. 7 2. 5 3. 6 4. 8 5. 8 6. 7 7. 8 8. 5
9. 6 10. 7 11. 6 12. 8 13. 5 14. 4

PAGE 67: 2. $1 + 4 + 4 = 9$
3. $2 + 1 + 2 = 5$
4. $1 + 1 + 1 + 2 = 5$
5. $4 + 1 + 1 + 4 = 10$
6. $3 + 1 + 2 = 6$
7. ART, RAT, or TAR $1 + 1 + 1 = 3$
8. BIKE $3 + 1 + 5 + 1 = 10$
9. ZOO $10 + 1 + 1 = 12$

PAGE 68: 1. $8 - 3 = 5$ 2. $3 - 2 = 1$
3. $4 - 3 = 1$ 4. $5 - 3 = 2$
5. $7 - 5 = 2$

PAGE 69: 1. $9 - 3 = 6$ 2. $5 - 4 = 1$
3. $8 - 5 = 3$ 4. $4 - 4 = 0$
5. $6 - 3 = 3$

PAGE 70: 1. 5 2. 5
3. 4 4. 5
5. 2 6. 4
7. 6 8. 2
9. 5 10. 6
11. 3 12. 6
13. 1 14. 7

PAGE 71: 1. $3 + 3 = 6$; $6 - 3 = 3$
2. $2 + 2 = 4$; $4 - 2 = 2$
3. $4 + 4 = 8$; $8 - 4 = 4$
4. $5 + 5 = 10$; $10 - 5 = 5$

PAGE 72: 1. picture 2 3. picture 1 3. picture 2 4. picture 1

PAGE 73: 1. g. 10 2. o. 5 3. f. 15 4. i. 5 5. s. 15
6. h. 10; GO FISH

PAGE 74: 1. 3 tens = 30 2. 5 tens = 50
3. 6 tens = 60 4. 4 tens = 40
5. 2 tens = 20 6. 7 tens = 70

PAGE 75: 1. 2 rods = 20 2. 4 rods = 4
3. 3 rods = 30 4. 9 rods = 90
5. 6 rods = 60

PAGE 76: 1. 50 2. 60 3. 60 4. 60 5. 90 6. 80
7. 50 8. 90 9. 50 10. 90 11. 90
12. 70 13. 80 14. 80

PAGE 77: 1. 5 tens, 3 ones = 53
2. 6 tens, 7 ones = 67
3. 4 tens, 6 ones = 46
4. 2 tens, 9 ones = 29
5. 3 tens, 5 ones = 35
6. 7 tens, 2 ones = 72

PAGE 78: 1. 3 tens, 2 ones 2. 4 tens, 6 ones
3. 6 tens, 4 ones 4. 8 tens, 1 one
5. 1 ten, 9 ones 6. 5 tens, 5 ones
7. 2 tens, 7 ones 8. 7 tens, 3 ones

PAGE 79: 1. 9 cents 2. 30 cents 3. 50 cents
4. 39 cents 5. 25 cents

PAGE 80: 1. 34 cents, whistle 2. 28 cents, ring
3. 45 cents, top 4. 64 cents, dinosaur

PAGE 81: 1. 2 dimes, 1 nickel — 25¢
2. 4 dimes, 5 pennies — 45¢
3. 6 nickels, 2 pennies — 32¢
4. 3 quarters — 75¢

PAGE 82: 2. 11 o'clock; 11:00
3. 5 o'clock; 5:00
4. 30 minutes after 4; 4:30
5. 30 minutes after 7; 7:30
6. 30 minutes after 10; 10:30

PAGE 83: 1. 30 minutes after 3; 3:30
2. 15 minutes after 12; 12:15
3. 45 minutes after 5; 5:45
4. 30 minutes after 10; 10:30
5. 45 minutes after 6; 6:45
6. 45 minutes after 11; 11:45

PAGE 84: *Personal answers*

PAGE 85: 1. 4 tens, 4 ones + 1 ten, 3 ones = 5 tens, 7 ones 2. 2 tens, 7 ones + 5 tens, 0 ones = 7 tens, 7 ones 3. 5 tens, 3 ones + 3 tens, 5 ones = 8 tens, 8 ones
4. 39 5. 86 6. 98 7. 57 8. 86

PAGE 86: *Clockwise from top:* 1. 25 (shown), 15, 55, 85, 35, 65 2. 84, 64, 95, 54, 74, 44 3. 68, 98, 28, 58, 88, 38 4. 47, 67, 97, 57, 37, 77

PAGE 87: 1. 14; $24 + 14 = 38$ 2. 11; $13 + 11 = 24$
3. 18; $21 + 18 = 39$ 4. 16; $32 + 16 = 48$
KAZOOS 19; $30 + 19 = 49$

PAGE 88: 1. 11 2. 21 3. 20 4. 41 5. 31 6. 23
7. 21 8. 21

PAGE 89: *Clockwise from upper-left section:*
1. 62 (shown), 72, 22, 2, 52, 32
2. 47, 27, 57, 17, 37, 7
3. 10, 50, 20, 42, 30, 60
4. 30, 20, 11, 6, 35, 34

PAGE 90: 1. 16 2. 79; 1 3. 14; 15 4. 12; same amount
5. Wendy with 77 points 6. 1

PAGE 91: 1. picture 3 2. picture 2 3. picture 1 4. picture 3

PAGE 92: *Personal answers*